Maimie in the Mobile

Maimie
in the
Mobile

By
Siân Lewin
& Georgina Lawson
Illustrated by Alex Robins

The special bond between a grandmother
and a grandchild is unbreakable,
no matter how much time may pass in between visits
or how many miles separate them.

With special thanks to my daughter Georgina,
who wrote the story with me,
and to my son-in-law Billy,
who was a great sounding board.

Imagination knows no bounds...

Daisy was playing in her bedroom; it was a warm and sunny afternoon in Australia.

Her favourite toys are her safari animals, she got them for her recent birthday.

They include a tall giraffe she's called Tilly, a lion called Louis, a zebra called Ace, plus Fanta the elephant.

Daisy loves to play with all her safari animals, but these are her favourite.

Suddenly, her mum popped her head around the bedroom door and said, "I am just going to bath your sister. If Maimie rings, will you answer my mobile and tell her I will call her back?"

Maimie is Daisy's grandma, who lives far away in England. Daisy loves chatting to Maimie on the mobile, she always makes her laugh.

A few moments later, the mobile rings. Daisy runs over to answer it and, sure enough, it's Maimie on the video.

"Hi, Maimie, how are you?" Daisy said.

"I am just tiddly-pom fantastic, how lovely to see you, what are you up to?" says Maimie.

"I'm playing with my safari animals, and they are looking for some water. I saw a programme about how far they must travel, so they can find some water to drink," explained Daisy.

"I know, it can be very hard. A few years ago, I went to the Serengeti National Park in Africa, in a country called Tanzania. It's a wonderful place, with so many beautiful animals."

"Oh, Maimie, that's so exciting, I would love to see all the animals there!" said Daisy.

"Well, if you put your hand on my hand and close your eyes really tightly, we will see what happens!" said Maimie.

Daisy's mum had always said that Maimie had some special powers! So, she put her hand on the mobile phone and shut her eyes very tightly...

Daisy felt a lovely warm glow and she opened her eyes, looked around and saw Maimie sitting next to her in a lovely old car.

"Welcome to Lottie, my special travel car, and a big welcome to the Serengeti!" beamed Maimie.

Daisy couldn't believe her eyes; she looked out of the window and saw lots of animals.

Daisy's four favourite toy animals
were also all in the car, peeping
out of the windows.

Daisy saw several giraffes, who looked just like Tilly. One had a baby giraffe with her.

"A baby giraffe is called a calf, and they are about six feet tall when they are born, just like your daddy!" said Maimie.

"When they are standing in a group, it's called a tower, and a moving group of giraffes is called a journey."

"Look, Tilly, there is your African family!" cried Daisy.

They drove a little further and saw a group of lions in the grasses.

"Lions are the only cats that live in groups. That is called a pride," said Maimie. "Do you know what baby lions are called, Daisy?"

"A cub, Maimie!" said Daisy, rather proudly.

"That's
tiddly-pom
fantastic, Daisy.
They also like to spend
twenty-one hours each day
resting and sleeping. I think
Maimie might like to be a lion!"

"I love the cubs, and that male lion
looks just like my Louis!" said Daisy.
Daisy took a big breath in and roared like
a lion. The little cub looked up and gave a little
roar back, which Daisy loved.

Lottie went a little further into the Serengeti and they came across some zebras. "Oh look, Ace, it's your family!" said a very excited Daisy.

"Now, a group of zebras is called a dazzle. They can be called a herd, but I think a dazzle is much more fun!" laughed Maimie.

"Ace loves seeing his cousins, Maimie, I think he wants to get out and run with them!" laughed Daisy.

Finally, they came across some elephants grazing in their herd by a pool.

"Looks like the elephants have found a nice pool to drink and play in," said Maimie! "Their trunks have a lot of muscles, sucking up the water to put in their mouths to drink.

They can hold up to ten litres of water in their trunk!

Plus they use it as a snorkel when swimming!"

At that moment, one of the elephants who had been drinking pointed his trunk towards Lottie the car and squirted her. Daisy squealed with delight and Maimie roared with laughter.

"Lottie is having a bath like my sister!" giggled Daisy. "Fanta, do you want to blow your trunk?"

"Now, that large elephant is giving Lottie a bit of a look, so I think it's time we left!"

"Thank you, Maimie, this has been fun!" said a rather excited Daisy.

Maimie drove Lottie safely and quickly away from the charging elephant. "I think he is just playing, but you can never be too sure!" smiled Maimie.

At that moment, Daisy felt the warm
glow again and her eyes closed. She felt
Maimie give her a hug and say, "Bye Daisy,
love you and see you soon. Next time maybe we
will see dinosaurs!"

"Daisy, Daisy, are you awake? You must have fallen asleep," said Daisy's mum.

Daisy opened her eyes slowly and smiled. "Yes, I've been to the Serengeti with Maimie in her special car, Lottie. We saw giraffes, lions, zebras and elephants!"

"Did Maimie tell you about her trips to Africa when she was a little girl?" said Daisy's mum.

"Oh no, Maimie really took me there and I'll tell you all about it, I've learnt so much!" smiled Daisy.

"I guess you are going to see dinosaurs next time with Maimie!" laughed her mum.

"How did you know?" said a surprised Daisy!

THE END

Printed in Great Britain
by Amazon

28833247R00016